WYND
WERRIBEE VIC 3030

P9-BBU-632

THIS BOOK BELONGS TO

PUFFIN BOOKS

Published by the Penguin Group
Melbourne • London • New York • Toronto • Dublin
New Delhi • Auckland • Johannesburg
Penguin Books Ltd, Registered Offices: 80 Strand, London WC2R 0RL, England
Published by Penguin Group (Australia), 2012
10 9 8 7 6 5 4 3 2 1
Text copyright © Davina Bell, 2012
Illustrations copyright © Lucia Masciullo, 2012
The moral right of the author and the illustrator has been asserted. All rights reserved.
Every effort has been made to contact the copyright holders for material used in this book.
If anyone has information on relevant copyright holders, please contact us.
Cover and internal design by Evi O. © Penguin Group (Australia)
Cover portrait © Tim de Neefe
Cover photograph © Rob Palmer
Printed and bound in Australia by McPherson's Printing Group, Maryborough, Victoria
National Library of Australia Cataloguing-in-Publication data available.
ISBN 978 0 14 330631 3

puffin.com.au
ouraustraliangirl.com.au

Charms on the front cover reprinted with kind permission from A&E Metal Merchants.
www.aemetals.com.au

MIX
Paper from
responsible sources
FSC
www.fsc.org
FSC® C001695

OUR
AUSTRALIAN
GIRL

Alice of Peppermint Grove

The war has finally ended. Alice
can't wait for Teddy to come home
from fighting in Europe so things
can go back to normal. But when
Mabel gets up to mischief and a
handsome stranger returns to
Peppermint Grove, life becomes
more complicated than ever. Can
Alice fix everyone's problems –
including her own?

Follow Alice on her adventure in
the third of four exciting stories
about a gifted girl in a time of
war.

Puffin Books

For you, Moge, because you are brave.
And for you, Gins, because you give me courage.

OUR
AUSTRALIAN
GIRL

Alice
of
Peppermint
Grove

Davina Bell

With illustrations by Lucia Masciullo

Puffin Books

AUSTRALIA

1918

Northern Territory

Western Australia

South

ALICE'S STORY

Alice struggles to keep her dreams of being a ballerina alive during World War One. Share in Alice's adventures as you read this story of a creative Australian girl.

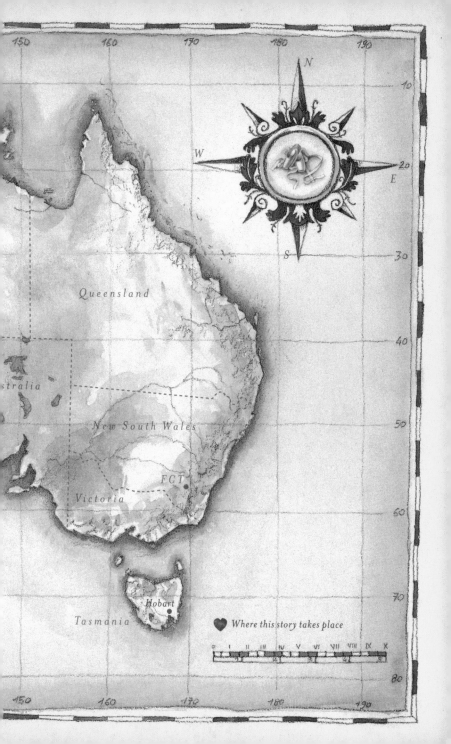

Queensland

New South Wales

ACT

Victoria

Hobart

Tasmania

Where this story takes place

THE STORY SO FAR

So many things have changed in Alice's life since the Great War began. Her father, Papa Sir, has been lost at sea; her brother Teddy has gone to fight in Europe; and Alice has given up dancing, along with her dreams of becoming a famous ballerina. But through all the ups and downs, one thing has stayed the same: it's been up to Alice to take care of everyone and hold the family together.

Now the war has ended, Christmas is coming, and Alice can't wait for Teddy to come home so life can go back to normal...

1
A LONG, HOT NIGHT

'A LICE?' whispered Mabel. 'Are you awake? I can't sleep – it's too hot.'

'Mmm, me neither,' Alice said to her sister, as she dripped water over her forehead. She and Mabel had dragged cot beds onto the top verandah, but even out in the open, it wasn't much cooler. The sea breeze hadn't come that afternoon and it felt as if Peppermint Grove was baking.

'Alice?' whispered Mabel. 'It's so hot I think I might die.'

'Mmm,' said Alice. 'Possibly.'

'Alice?' whispered Mabel. 'I –'

'Well, what do you expect me to do about it?' Alice snapped, turning over to glare at Mabel. But Mabel looked strange – she almost seemed frightened. Alice couldn't remember the last time Mabel had been frightened of anything.

'Sorry,' Alice whispered, 'it's awful when it's like this, I know.' She held out her hand. Mabel took it, and they lay there for a minute.

'Alice? I did something silly,' Mabel began again after a pause. 'I need your help.'

Alice let go of Mabel's hand and sat up. 'What did you do? Of course I'll help.'

'I . . . Oh, I can't tell you. I'm too ashamed.' Mabel turned and buried her face in her pillow. 'It's bad.'

Alice was itching to know, but she just said calmly, 'Everyone makes mistakes. There's nothing that can't be put right. Count to ten, take a deep breath and just say it.'

In the pause that followed, she tried to imagine what Mabel was going to say. Well, she can't have killed anyone, Alice thought. Perhaps she's broken something – Grandmama's crystal glasses?

'I told a lie. A big lie. Lots of lies,' Mabel whispered.

'What do you mean? To who?'

'I've been writing letters to a soldier. Pretending I'm a lady.'

'Oh Mabel,' said Alice, exasperated. 'Why would you do that? Did he write back?'

Mabel turned over and nodded, sniffing. 'Lots of times. We've been writing for months.'

'Well, that was a silly thing to do. Really, Mabel, I know you probably thought it was funny, but lies always hurt someone. What did you tell him about yourself? Your imaginary self, I mean.'

'Oh . . . you know . . . things . . . That I only wore yellow, and that I had an identical twin and that I played the trombone. Things like that.'

'The *trombone*?'

Mabel nodded, wiping at her nose. 'Because I told him I have big lips. Oh – and that my name was Arabella. That I only have champagne for breakfast. And I might have said that I was very funny.'

Alice groaned. 'Did Violet put you up to this? No, don't even tell me how the whole thing came about. Look, I won't tell anyone, but you've got to write and tell him the truth.'

Mabel shook her head. 'You don't understand. James – that's the soldier – he's coming back and he wants to meet me. At the Indiana Tea House.'

Alice lay down again. The backs of her knees felt raw with being so sweaty, and somewhere near her ear, a mosquito whined.

'Alice?' whispered Mabel. 'Will you come with me to meet him? He sounds so nice that I can't leave him sitting there waiting. Can I stand on your shoulders and put a coat over you so I look like I'm twenty? *Please*, Alice?'

'*What?* That's ridiculous. Mabel, you're just so –' But then Alice reminded herself that with Teddy still away at war and Papa Sir gone forever, it was up to her to fix things, and being horrid about it wouldn't make life any easier. 'There's nothing else for it – we'll have to go and meet him, and apologise *lots*, and use your pocket money to buy him tea.'

'What – all of it?'

'Mabel!'

'All right, all right. But what if he gets violent? You know what some of those soldiers are like – they're deranged.'

'It's not their fault! You would be, too, if you'd had to hear bombs exploding all day and all night, and you couldn't sleep, and you'd been up to your ankles in mud.'

'Stop it!' Mabel said, her voice starting to go scratchy with tears.

Alice clicked her tongue. 'Oh, don't cry. If he's nice in his letters, I don't think he'll be violent. At least, not in a tea house.' She covered her eyes. 'When is this horrible meeting exactly?'

'The day after tomorrow.'

'*The day after tomorrow?*'

'At two. I said I'd wear yellow so he could recognise me.'

'But you don't own anything yellow!'

'I know. Could we make something, Alice? Perhaps we could boil up some dye and colour a sheet or something?'

'Please don't talk to me right now,' said Alice, turning her back to Mabel and kicking the covers off her bed. 'And as soon as we get home from the beach tomorrow, I'm boiling *you* in yellow dye.'

2

ON COTTESLOE BEACH

'**E**VEN though the nights can be awful, summer's still my favourite season,' said Alice to her best friend Jilly, as they lay under the pine trees on the slope overlooking Cottesloe Beach the next day. She propped herself up on one elbow to make sure she could still see her sisters, Mabel and Pudding and Little, digging their monster sandcastle in the shallows below.

It was such perfect beach weather that Alice had been able to push the awful meeting with the soldier right out of her mind. She and Jilly had stayed in the turquoise water all morning, until the pads of their fingertips wrinkled.

Now they were lying on the grass under the huge trees where George had spent the whole day reading and guarding the picnic basket. Even though it was almost evening, the sea breeze still hadn't come, and without the stinging sand it blew up, they'd been able to stay all afternoon in the dry warmth that Alice loved. She felt tingling pink and crusted with salt and very, very happy. 'Yes, mine's definitely summer,' she said. 'What's yours?'

'Summer's too hot for me,' said Jilly, 'and I get too many freckles. I like autumn.'

'But after autumn it's dreary winter! And in summer there's so much to do, and it's Christmas and holidays, and you can swim at the beach or the river baths and it doesn't get dark till late, so you can –'

'That's the problem with you, Alice,' said George, as he turned a page. 'You're always trying to change everyone's minds.'

'Am not. I'm just saying that there are lots of good things about summer.'

'Mosquitoes buzzing all through the night? Heat stroke? Sunburn? Sand down your bathing costume?' George scoffed. 'I like winter, myself. Lots of time for indoor pursuits – reading, quiet reflection, writing my opus . . .'

Alice groaned. 'Not your wretched opus. If you start on your opus again, I'll fold you up and stuff you into that picnic basket.'

'What's an opus?' asked Jilly.

'Just a fancy word for a big piece of work – a big bit of writing or music or something. George has discovered Shakespeare.' Alice sighed. 'You know, the Englishman who wrote all the plays, and –'

'The Bard,' said George. 'Born in 1564. The greatest writer who ever lived. I'm composing a series of theatrical pieces as a tribute to his genius. Would you be interested in being part of my troupe of actors, Jilly?'

'Oh – I, er . . . it's more Alice's sort of thing, isn't it? I think I'd be too shy.'

'You could be a tree, perhaps. I'll need a few of those for my tragedy, *The Garden of Good and Evil*.'

'Good grief, George,' said Alice. 'I think Jilly has better things to do than stand around while you boss her about the angles of her branches. Ah – here comes the breeze.'

Above them, the long, springy branches of the Norfolk pine trees started to bounce a little, and then a cool, light wind was swishing through everything, making it fresh again. It was called the Fremantle Doctor because it made everything better. Just like Papa Sir used to do, Alice thought, and he was a doctor, too.

But Papa Sir had been lost at sea in the war in Europe that had just finished. When all the soldiers came home, he wouldn't be among them, waving and smiling as his ship pulled up to the docks at Fremantle. Alice's heart still felt bruised whenever she let herself remember. At least you'll have Teddy, she reminded herself. He'll be here soon. Alice felt she could stand anything if Teddy, her big brother, was beside her.

'Have you had any word about when your papa will be back from the war?' she asked Jilly. 'And Hamish?' Hamish was Jilly's oldest brother, who had been away almost since the start of the fighting four years ago.

'Well, I heard the other day that the first ones to join up are going to be the first ones home, so it won't be that long, after all.'

'What do you mean?' asked Alice. 'Won't they just come home together?'

Jilly shook her head. 'The railways in France and Belgium are all clogged up with people, and there aren't enough spare ships to send the soldiers all at once. Some will have to wait a few months.'

'Oh,' said Alice. Teddy had been one of the

last to leave – he'd only been in France for a few months before the peace agreement had been signed. It might be ages before he was home, and by then it would be winter again, and they wouldn't be able to play tennis or go out on Papa Sir's boat. They'd have to sit inside listening to George's opus and . . . Alice caught herself frowning. You're lucky that Teddy's coming home at all, she told herself sternly.

'Must you be back soon, Jilly?' she asked.

'Mother lets me stay out as long as I like now. Come over and have tea with us, and you can see for yourself how much she's changed.'

'That would be lovely,' Alice murmured. But she didn't mean it. She was still frightened of Mrs McNair, and angry with her.

Up until a month ago, Mrs McNair had been the strictest mother alive – as strict as a gaol guard. For weeks, she hadn't allowed Jilly and Alice to see each other at all.

But then Jilly's brother Douglas had been

caught doing horrible things around the town. And even though it was because fighting in the war had hurt his mind, Mrs McNair had felt very ashamed and blamed herself. Now she let Jilly do almost as she liked, and Alice and Jilly had spent most of the holidays together. It was only the week before Christmas, so there were weeks of holidays to come, stretching before them like a magic road.

'Guess what, Alice? She's even said I can start ballet again in the new year. You could start again, too – we could do it together.'

In a second, Alice felt her stomach twist up in a big, uncomfortable knot. She opened one eye to squint at Jilly. 'You know I'm not dancing anymore, Jilly. It's different for me. It's trickier.'

'Just because you said that once, doesn't mean you have to hold by it forever. Miss Josephine is taking the classes, in case you change your mind. She's not Miss Lillibet, I know, but I've heard she's nice. Think about it, anyway.'

Thinking about ballet was something Alice tried hard not to do. That was why she loved summer – you could fill the days with outdoorsy things so you didn't have to think about the letter hidden under your mattress that said you could be the best ballerina in the world. 'Shall we fly the kite now the breeze is in?' she asked, sitting up.

Jilly grinned. 'Don't think I haven't noticed you change the subject. But we may as well – we brought it all this way.'

'George, we'll be back as soon as the sun's down,' said Alice.

George looked up. 'I do find the ocean sunset a particularly productive time for my writing,' he said gravely. 'As did the poet Shelley. We should come here every evening.'

'Sometimes George is so ridiculous,' Alice said as they skipped along the path to a point high enough to launch their kite.

'You never know, he could be a famous writer

some day. Just as you could be a famous dancer.'

Alice sighed as she unwound the string from the spool. 'Jilly, I said I wouldn't dance anymore because I felt like it made me selfish. And with Papa Sir gone now, it's my job to take care of everyone. I don't have time for ballet.'

She handed the kite to Jilly, who did the run-up and launched it into the sky. They watched it climb up and out and up and out until it looked as if it were higher than the sun, which sat on the line of the ocean like a ball of gold.

'You won't like hearing this, Alice,' said Jilly carefully, 'but taking care of everyone isn't your job – at least, not yours alone. And besides, for someone as good at ballet as you, couldn't dancing be your job?'

Was Jilly right? Alice wasn't sure. She looked out at the huge orange sky and the silvery sea that stretched across to Africa. The war had changed so many things that she wasn't sure of much anymore.

3

JAMES BUSBY-WILKS

THE next morning, Alice and Mabel didn't have to dye anything because Mabel found a lemon-yellow party dress in the dress-up box. The front was covered in tiny glass beads that sparkled like crystal. Alice thought it was completely ridiculous, but she was getting so worried about the whole thing that she didn't argue, and even tacked the hem up so Mabel could walk in it.

As Alice quickly did the lunch dishes while she waited for Mabel to choose some shoes, Mama swept in and dropped her handbag and a newspaper onto the kitchen table.

'Mama! Why aren't you at work?' Alice asked in surprise.

'*Bonjour, ma petite.* I 'ave the rest of the day off. Where is everyone?'

'Pudding's gone with Uncle Bear to see Mr Logue – Little's gone, too. George is up a tree, thinking about his opus. And Mabel and I are off to the seaside.'

'An outing?' Mama said as she sat down. 'I shall join you! You know I adore the seaside.'

'Oh – ahh, I think . . . sorry, Mama, it's a special sisters' outing,' said Alice, feeling mean but not wanting Mabel to be embarrassed. 'I promised Mabel we'd do something, just us.'

Mama stuck out her lip. '*D'accord*, I will stay home like Cinderella, weeping and sewing in my rags.'

She scowled and unfolded the newspaper. But after a few moments she stood up again and stalked around the kitchen. She seemed tense and springy, not her breezy self at all.

'Is something wrong, Mama?' Alice asked as she set the last dish in the drying rack.

'This flu – it is everywhere,' Mama said, pointing to the paper crossly. 'It is spreading like a fire. These poor soldiers – they survive months and years of fighting, and then *poof!* The Spanish flu, it kills them in days. *C'est pas juste* – it is not fair.'

'But not here – not in Australia. It's only in Europe and America, isn't it?'

George had told them all about the Spanish flu when he'd tried to look it up in Papa Sir's medical encyclopedia. He'd said that you could catch it in the morning and be dead by nightfall – that it had already killed more people than the whole war – and predicted that none of them would still be alive by the new year. 'When you bleed from your ears,' he'd said grimly, 'you know that's that.'

But thankfully the new year was less than

a fortnight away, and so far there had been no cases of the Spanish flu in Western Australia.

Mama paused at the big kitchen window, looking out at the white sails of the boats on Freshwater Bay, flapping like big handkerchiefs. '*Oui.*' She sighed. 'But that is not what is on my mind,' she said eventually. 'Mr Peterkins is home from the war.'

Mr Peterkins had been the manager at the bank. Mama had replaced him when he'd joined the air force – he was a friend of Papa Sir's, and knew that she was a wizard with numbers, so he'd given her the job.

'That's good, isn't it?' asked Alice. 'That means you won't have to work as hard.'

'It means I will not 'ave to work at all,' said Mama bitterly. 'I am no longer needed.'

'Oh. Well, couldn't you get another job?'

Mama shook her head. 'The soldiers who are coming 'ome need to work too, *n'est ce pas*? And so the women must give up their jobs –

it will be happening everywhere. But *ma petite*, what shall I do? This job, it showed me that I love to work. And I am just as good as a man! *Mon Dieu* – my God, I shall be bored. Per'aps I will take up golf.'

But Alice couldn't imagine that. Mama liked doing things: busy things or beautiful things.

'You could take up something new,' Alice suggested. 'You could train for the Swim-Through! It's going to be so exciting.'

For the past couple of weeks, Peppermint Grove had been humming with the news of the Swim-Through – the first-ever swimming race across Mosman Bay. It wasn't until March, but already people were training each morning, cutting across the water with slick, quick strokes.

'Splashing about in the cold? *Tiens!* I would sooner kiss a spotted pig.'

Mabel and Alice set off down Forrest Street, and soon they were walking against the crowds that had come from the railway station at Cottesloe with their baskets and puppies and empty kerosene tins for catching crabs. All summer long, people journeyed to Peppermint Grove from miles around to spend the day on the foreshore, picnicking and swimming and sailing in little boats. But we don't even have to catch a train or a ferry; we only have to walk down the hill, thought Alice dreamily, and it's all here; it's all ours.

As they crossed over the railway line and started up the hill, however, Alice began to feel nervous. At the very least, this man would think they were fools. At worst, he could, well, he could do anything. Break cake plates over their heads. But as Mabel marched along, admiring how the glass beads shimmered on her dress, her fear from the night before last seemed to have completely vanished.

As they got to the crest of the hill, Cottesloe Beach stretched out before them, and immediately Alice felt calm again. Today, the water was bright blue – a blue as strong as cornflowers – and it made Alice feel strong, too. The beach and the tall pine trees always reminded her of Papa Sir, who had brought her here every weekend in the summers before he'd left for war. As she and Mabel walked into the Indiana Tea House, Alice had the feeling that Papa Sir was with her and things would be all right.

The tea house wasn't a posh tea room; it was more like a big tin shed with a long row of windows along the seafront, so you could see the ocean. You'd get a beautiful view of the sunset, Alice thought. When Teddy comes back, we should bring him here so he can paint it.

The big space was bustling with people, and Alice looked around for a soldier sitting alone at a table. 'What does he look like?' she whispered.

'I've no idea,' Mabel whispered back. 'Shall I stand on a seat and call his name?'

'*No.*'

'There! By the window, in the uniform. I bet that's him,' she said, striding off. 'Excuse me, please,' she demanded, before Alice had even reached the table.

The soldier's fingernails were black and his hair was greasy, and as he looked up from stirring his tea, his eyes were red and narrow. As he took in Mabel and the yellow dress, his lip curled up, and something about him looked hungry.

'Sorry sir,' Alice said. 'I think we've got the wrong person. Come along, Mabel.'

'How do you know what sort of person I am if you don't sit down?' he said. 'Come now, girls, keep a soldier company.'

'Sorry, but we're looking for someone special,' said Mabel, starting to back away.

The soldier flicked out his hand and caught Mabel by the wrist. 'I'm special,' he whispered.

The sight of Mabel's little wrist in his big grubby hand made Alice's throat burn with sick. She grabbed hold of Mabel's other arm. 'I'm sure you are, sir, it's just that we have to –'

'Don't move and don't scream,' snarled the soldier quietly, standing up.

'Cousins! My dear little cousins – you're here,' came a kindly voice from behind them, and they all turned to see a tall man sitting at a table for two, spinning a straw boater on his finger. 'Thank you, officer, for bringing me the rascals. Come girls, I've been waiting an age to order tea.'

Alice didn't have any cousins – at least, none in Australia – but she realised suddenly that the tall, kindly man was trying to help them. She swallowed. 'Hello, Cousin . . . Jimmy.'

The soldier glared, but as he took in Cousin Jimmy's wide chest and broad shoulders, he let

Mabel's wrist go and walked away, muttering to himself.

'Are you all right?' asked the man who wasn't really Cousin Jimmy. 'Do you need to sit down a moment?'

Alice felt herself start to tremble. But Mabel, who had been pale as pale a moment before, brushed back her hair and forged on. 'We're looking for someone called James Busby-Wilks. Do you know him?'

'I am him,' said the kind man, looking curious.

Before he could even stand up to hold out his hand, Mabel plonked herself onto the seat opposite him and leaned forward.

'Here's the thing. I'm Arabella – well, I'm not, obviously, but my sister wouldn't let me stand on her shoulders under a coat. I wrote the letters and yes, I'm a big liar, and if you're going to get violent, I'll have you know that my brother's also a soldier, and he'll be home soon and probably thump you. And by the way, I'm not twenty,

I'm eight. And my name's Mabel.' She paused
to draw breath and picked up the menu. 'Now
we've got that out of the way, have you ordered
any refreshments? Oh – and that's Alice.'

Alice and James Busby-Wilks stared at each
other, completely bewildered. Just at that
moment, a waitress in a frilled apron came
over with another chair. 'For you, ma'am,' she
said to Alice. 'Now, what can I get for you
folks?'

'Tea for all,' said Mabel. 'And possibly a plate
of lamingtons . . . If that's all right, James?'

'Ye-es,' James stammered, his eyes wide. He
swallowed. 'That sounds very nice indeed.'

The waitress took the menus, and Alice sat
down and took a deep breath, her legs jittering
under the table. 'Mr Busby-Wilks, I'm really
truly sorry to tell you, especially as you just
saved our lives, but I only learned last night
that Mabel has been . . . misleading you. You
see, she's been writing you letters pretending

to be someone else, because . . . actually, I have no idea why. Mabel?'

'Lots of ladies write to soldiers they don't know. It's romantic.'

'You're not a lady! You're a child!' Alice rolled her eyes.

'But I write just as well as any lady, don't I, James?'

Mabel had a point – she was very good at composition.

Any shock that James felt had been smoothed from his friendly face. He nodded. 'You had me utterly convinced. You have a lovely way with words, Mabel.'

Alice felt relieved. 'So you're not going to break a plate on our heads? Oh – I didn't mean to say that out loud. Sorry,' she said, feeling her neck get hot.

'Not at all. I save my plate-breaking for special occasions – birthdays, Christmas, that sort of thing.'

Mabel giggled as the tea and cakes arrived and were passed around.

Alice frowned. 'But how did Mabel write to you if she didn't even know you?'

Mabel blushed as James pulled an envelope out of his pocket. '*To the handsomest boy in the 48th Battalion*' it said in her flowery writing.

'Were you really the handsomest?' asked Alice.

Mabel snorted. 'Of course he was – look at him.'

'Mabel!' said Alice. 'Sorry, sir – my sister has no manners.'

James looked sheepish. 'The fellows in my squadron took a vote and decided the letter was for me.'

As Alice took in James properly – his blue eyes with their long lashes and his honey-coloured hair and smooth, brown skin, and the way only one of his cheeks dimpled when he smiled – she decided that she would have given him the letter, too.

'And we've been writing ever since, haven't we, Mabel,' said James, picking up his teacup in his big hand, and sipping it gently. 'Thank you so much for your letters. In dark hours, they gave me hope.'

Alice thought it was nice of James to be grateful, given that Mabel had told the most jumbo lies. 'You're English,' she said, recognising James's crisp accent. 'Our father is English. Was English,' she corrected herself.

'*Actually*,' said Mabel, 'James is from here. It's just that before the war he lived in England for a bit, playing professional croquet.'

James smiled. 'Not croquet – professional cricket. Yes, I fancied myself a batsman for a while, and Father was good enough to let me go over there and try it out.'

'Is that what you're going to do now?' Alice asked. 'Play cricket, I mean?'

James looked at her thoughtfully. Alice had a feeling that she'd never had before; that she'd quite like James to reach out and put his palm against her cheek, and hold it there – perhaps forever. Good grief, thought Alice, horrified. If I'm not careful, I'll start writing awful love poetry, like Jilly.

He lifted up his left hand, which he'd been resting on his knee – at least, that's what Alice had assumed. But as he leaned his left arm on the table, Alice saw that there was no hand at the end of his sleeve, which had been pinned shut.

'Cricket's out of the question, I'm afraid,' he said, and though his voice was matter-of-fact, his eyes looked sad and wishful.

'Why did you come back to WA – if you have no family here, I mean?' asked Mabel, completely unfussed by a missing hand. She turned to Alice. 'His father died while he was away, and he hasn't anyone else. I know from the letters.'

James looked down at his plate and blushed, and suddenly Alice had a terrible thought:

perhaps he'd come back for the beautiful, funny, trombone-playing Arabella he thought Mabel was. I bet he wanted to marry her, Alice realised, feeling as if her heart would melt for poor, handsome James. And now he had nobody. 'Sorry, James – I mean, sir. It was rude of Mabel to ask,' she said.

'Not at all, Alice – and please, do call me James.' He leaned back in his seat, and looked out the big windows to where the cornflower sea met the soft white sand. 'I suppose after all those years in England I missed the sunshine. And things are tough in London. The place is crawling with men who are in a bad way. Shell shock's an awful thing.'

'What's shell shock?' asked Mabel.

'It's something that soldiers get in battle, isn't it?' asked Alice, thinking back to a conversation she'd overheard at the Post Office about Douglas McNair. 'It's what makes them go a little strange.'

'Precisely,' said James. 'Poor fellows.' He popped some lamington into his mouth. 'Mm, good choice, Mabel. Also, I heard they're going to open up the whole south-west of the state for returned soldiers to farm – give them land to grow things. I liked the sound of that. Even with my hand gone, I think I could grow fruit trees – apples, peaches, plums, apricots. And, well, I guess I'd like to have a family of my own some day. I'll need some busy little hands to help me pick all that fruit.'

'We've got fruit trees in our orchard,' said Mabel happily as Alice imagined James smiling down at a bunch of flaxen-haired children out in a sun-soaked field. 'You should come and see them. If you can stand on a ladder, you can get some apricots down for Little – that's our sister. She makes jam. *Can* you balance on a ladder, do you think, or would you fall off? It might be hard with only a stump.'

Alice was about to kick Mabel under the table when she saw that James was struggling not to laugh. 'Yes, come around and meet our mother,' she said, feeling that she couldn't bear to say goodbye to James just yet. 'Are you free on Christmas Eve? That's when we have our Christmas dinner because Mama's French. Would you like to join us?'

'As it happens, I have no plans. Your mother wouldn't mind?' he asked.

'Not at all. About six o'clock? We're at the corner of Forrest and View Streets.'

'Two of my favourite things.'

'We'd best be going,' said Alice, nudging Mabel's foot under the table to remind her about paying. But Mabel just glared and kicked her back.

'Thank you, girls, for coming to meet me and explain,' said James. 'You could have left me sitting here, always wondering what might have been with the alluring Arabella.'

'I'm sorry we weren't what you expected,' said Alice.

'You were delightful company. The pleasure was all mine.'

'Mabel has something to say,' Alice said, looking at her pointedly.

'Yes,' said Mabel. 'You're every bit as nice as you were in your letters.'

'*No*, Mabel, I mean about the –'

'Be off before you make a man blush,' said James. 'I'll see you on Christmas Eve.'

'That went well, didn't it,' said Mabel, as she and Alice ran up the hill away from the beach.

'It certainly did *not*,' said Alice. 'We almost got kidnapped! And you were supposed to pay to say sorry – that was the whole point.'

'Really, Alice, either way you would have got a nice free tea, so I don't know what you're so het up about. You should actually be thanking me for introducing you to the handsomest man alive. Perhaps you should have bought *me* the refreshments.'

Alice clenched her fists. 'You're unbelievable, Mabel.' How on earth are we even related? she fumed as they marched home in silence. Mabel just does as she likes and doesn't even think about how anyone else feels. And yet everything in her life turns out just fine.

But a tiny part of Alice wondered if it mightn't be rather nice to not worry so much about everyone all the time – to not always be the stick-in-the-mud, trying to make things all right.

When they got home, yet another surprise awaited them: Mama – who never cooked – was in the kitchen whisking egg whites and sugar in the baking bowl. Pudding and Little and George were gathered around her, taking turns to dip their fingers into the mixture.

'Alice!' said Little. 'I've something to tell you!'

The pretty pink spots on her small cheeks made Alice suddenly want to kiss them. 'That you're really the child of a fairy and an elf, and at night you sleep under a giant mushroom?'

Little frowned. '*No*. When I was in Claremont with Pudding and Uncle Bear this morning, we thought we saw Miss Lillibet in the distance. But we were late for Mr Logue, so we couldn't run after her, and she was quite far away. Might she be home, Mama?'

Alice felt hope come swooping inside her as she thought of beautiful Miss Lillibet being amongst them once more. But it left almost as quickly as it had come when she remembered that she would have to tell Miss Lillibet she had given up dancing forever.

'Well, the war is over now,' said Mama thoughtfully as she tipped her mixture into the piping bag. 'Germany 'as lost. It makes sense that they let the German people out of the camps. But I have 'eard that lots of them are being sent back to Germany – even the ones who have never been there before. *C'est fou!* It's crazy.'

Alice frowned and ran her finger along the inside of the bowl. 'You mean even people who were born here but whose relatives are German, like Miss Lillibet?' Poor Miss Lillibet, she thought. I don't think she even speaks German. She won't know anybody. 'That's the stupidest thing I've ever heard.'

'The fighting is over, but still people clutch onto their fears, *non*?' said Mama.

'But we won the war, so why go on being horrid to the Germans? It doesn't make sense. People should just forgive each other.'

For some reason, the face of Mrs McNair flickered in Alice's mind, and she felt a pang of guilt. You too, Alice, she said to herself.

'Mama, we made a new friend today at

the beach – a soldier,' said Alice, suddenly remembering. 'He's called James. We invited him to Christmas dinner. Is that all right? He doesn't have any family left.'

'And he's only got one hand,' said Mabel, 'but he's devilishly handsome.'

'*Quelle triste* – 'ow sad! Yes, of course 'e must come. And for this James, I will do a special Christmas dessert – a French masterpiece,' said Mama.

'Are you sure?' asked Alice uncertainly. 'We could just have meringues again – you're good at those.'

'Or Little could make her trifle,' suggested Mabel.

Mama smiled and wagged her finger. 'Aaah, you 'ave doubts! You think your *maman* is not a chef! You will see, *mes enfants*. From where do you think Little has got 'er talents?'

4
CHRISTMAS EVE

CHRISTMAS had been Papa Sir's favourite time of year, and this was the first one since they had found out that he was most probably dead. But with Mama home and full of happy plans, the days leading up to Christmas weren't sad and sombre, as Alice had feared. They were magical.

Mabel had found a record of Christmas carols and played it non-stop on the gramophone. The house smelled like baking, and each day there were new stories of the peace – of soldiers meeting their babies for the first time, or returning home when their families had given up hope. It looked as if the Spanish flu would skip Western Australia altogether, and that alone was a reason to celebrate.

But when the doorbell rang on Christmas Eve, Alice suddenly felt a little nervous. What if James thought her family was strange? They were a little, if you thought about it. 'He's here, everyone,' she called.

'Just finishing off this scene,' George called back from Papa Sir's study.

Everyone else filed into the hall as Mabel bolted past them to the front door.

'Good evening, Miss Arabella,' James said with a wink as she opened it. 'Hello there, Alice.'

'James,' Mabel said breathily, holding out her hand for him to kiss, 'this is my mother, Marie-Claire – can you shake hands, James? Oh yes – it's only your left one that's gone. And this is Little, she made almost all the food even though she's small, and Pudding's in the garden, riding the goat – that's not her real name, in case you were wondering – and George is coming, he's just working on his opus, and that's Uncle Bear, and he doesn't talk but he's the cleverest man I know. Except Papa Sir, of course, but he passed away.'

'*Enchanté*,' said Mama. 'Enchanted to meet you.'

'Sorry, sir,' said George, as he rushed in and stuck out his hand. 'I was just –'

'Working on your opus, I understand. Good to meet you, George.'

'Come through, James,' said Alice, leading him through the parlour and out the back. 'It's such a nice evening that we're going to eat outside on the terrace. Pudding, come and meet James! Unhitch Tatty's cart and tie him to the tree, please.'

'So, what are you writing, George?' James asked as they all sat down and put the special lace serviettes onto their laps, and Uncle Bear helped Little carry out the last of the dishes.

'A series of theatrical pieces inspired by the works of –'

'Don't say it,' said Alice and Mabel together.

'The Bard,' George went on.

'Shakespeare,' said James. 'Finest writer who ever lived. My favourite. You know, my father was a writer.'

'Really?' said George.

'What kind of writer?' asked Mama as she elegantly sliced the goose with a very long knife.

'Thank you, Little,' said James, accepting a dish of cheesy potato gratin. 'This all looks delicious. He wrote books – novels, actually. He was also a reverend, so he wrote under a different name and nobody ever guessed.'

'Would we know him?' asked Alice.

'Perhaps. I'm sorry – this is very rude of me, coming here and only talking about myself.'

They all protested – of course it wasn't.

'Who is it? Do tell us,' insisted Mabel. 'Is it someone famous?'

'I wouldn't go that far, but I think you might have heard of him. His books are for children, but adults seem to like them just as much. He writes as Babington Wilder.'

They gasped – everyone except Pudding, who was the only one who couldn't read, and had her mouth full of potato.

'Babington Wilder,' said Alice with awe. 'He *is* famous. He's our very favourite author.'

'Except for The Bard,' said George, 'though their styles are very different, so perhaps it's accurate to say that he is our favourite novelist, and Shakespeare is our favourite playwright.'

'*Your* favourite playwright,' said Mabel.

'*Alors!*' said Mama with feeling. 'We 'ave read them all! *Sunward I Have Climbed* and *Come Home, Mrs Cloud* . . .'

'*The Castle of Good Mr Malmsberry*. But my

best is *Hope and the Wide, Bright Sky*,' said Alice. 'When the mother died, I cried for a week.'

'That's my favourite, too,' said James. 'Father wrote it about my mother dying. Though obviously the bit with the flying boy wasn't real. At least, I don't think it was, anyway.'

'Oh, I'm sorry for bringing it up,' said Alice. 'That must have been awful.'

'But now it's been turned into a beautiful story, and my mother would have been happy about that,' said James.

They all had a thousand questions for James, and he didn't mind answering them a bit. And he knew exactly the part of Paris where Mama had grown up, and he talked to George all about iambic pentameter and cinquains. As the feast went on, Alice thought he looked more and more . . . what was the word? Not surprised, not pleased but *enchanté* – enchanted, just as Mama had said. Alice felt relieved.

As Little started to clear the plates and Mama brought out her grand dessert, James lifted Pudding up and put her on his shoulders and galloped around the garden, just the way she loved. That was what he was doing when Miss Lillibet walked around the corner in her long, white skirt.

'Hello?' she called. 'Here you all are! Oh dear – I hope I'm not interrupting your Christmas dinner.'

'Miss Lillibet!' cried Alice, as she and all the girls ran over, launching themselves at Miss Lillibet so that she was almost knocked down with love.

'*Ma cherie*,' Mama cried. 'You are just in time for my triumphant dessert. A *Bûche de Noël* – a log of Christmas. Come, meet our new friend, and we will all be merry together.'

'Miss Lillibet, come and meet James – his papa is Babington Wilder!' said Mabel. 'Don't mind his missing hand.'

'Oh Miss Lillibet, merry merry Christmas!' said Alice, kissing her teacher on both cheeks. 'So you don't have to go and live in Germany?'

'No, I don't have to live in Germany,' said Miss Lillibet, 'though lots of people I was with in the camp have been sent there. Hello, I'm Lily – or Miss Lillibet, whichever you prefer.' She held out her dainty hand to James, and he took it and bowed his head, and Alice thought that Miss Lillibet was just as pretty as before she'd been sent away to the camp – maybe even prettier – and that's when a big plan hatched in her mind; the kind of plan that made her stomach tight with happiness.

'I'm James. And I'm going to call you Lily, just to be original.'

Miss Lillibet laughed. 'You're the son of Babington Wilder – could you be anything else? I'm a huge admirer.'

'Miss Lillibet,' said Pudding from up on James's shoulders.

Miss Lillibet leaned forward, her mouth open. 'Well I never, Pudding, you clever thing. You've learned to speak!'

'Yes,' said Pudding shyly. 'With Lionel.'

'Lionel Logue – that's her speech therapist,' said Mabel. 'Miss Lillibet, tell us all about the camp. Was it awful?'

'Mabel! This is not polite. You do not 'ave to say a word if you would rather not,' said Mama, passing Miss Lillibet a cup.

'No, no, I'm perfectly happy to speak of it. Well, Mabel, it was . . . difficult. And sad. And uplifting. All at the same time.'

'What was uplifting about it?' asked Alice. 'Wasn't it a prison?'

'In some ways, and the lack of freedom – well, that was truly horrible. To walk around now wherever I like feels as if I have wings.' She sipped her tea. 'But there were good things, too – brave things; people coming together and making the most of an awful situation. Some of the internees had set up a theatre group, and a choir, and a shop. I saw Wagner's operas sung in German by people with the love of their home in their hearts.' Miss Lillibet's eyes brimmed with tears. 'But there were also people like me – people whose grandparents or even great-grandparents were German, but who'd never been to Germany and didn't speak the language. It seemed so silly that we were locked away when we were no threat to the war. So there was anger, too. Yes, it was such a mixture of things, I feel as though I may never understand it,' she said, looking off into the distance. 'But come now, tell me your news! I hear that you're waiting for Teddy to return, is that right?'

'Probably not for a while,' said Alice.

'Teddy's our brother,' said Mabel to James.

'The one with the big muscles who was going to thump me?' he said, his eyes full of mischief.

'Teddy couldn't thump a drum,' said Miss

Lillibet, smiling. 'He's an artist – a beautiful painter. I do hope he's well.'

'And Miss Lillibet is a ballerina – a *very* good one,' said Alice proudly. 'You can probably tell because she's so graceful. She's also a dance teacher.' Then suddenly Alice remembered all the things that Miss Lillibet didn't know, and she wished that she hadn't brought it up.

'No longer, I'm afraid,' said Miss Lillibet.

'*Mais non! Pour quoi* – why?' asked Mama.

Miss Lillibet sat back in her chair, rubbing her fingertips over her forehead. 'It seems that even though the war is over, the local women aren't comfortable with me teaching their children. Apparently I'm still the enemy. So I'm at rather a loss about what to do with myself. Besides teaching you, of course, Alice.'

'*Actually* . . .' said Mabel.

Alice felt shame bloom inside her. But she made herself look straight into her teacher's brown eyes. 'Miss Lillibet? I've . . . I'm not dancing anymore. Because . . . because of everything. I can't talk about it this minute, if that's all right with you.'

'Oh, Alice,' said Miss Lillibet, and her face filled with sadness.

In the big pause that followed, they could hear the soft clinks of the anchored boats on the river, knocking against their chains.

'Are you very disappointed in me?' Alice whispered.

'My dear child . . . It's just . . . all the time I was locked away, I −' Miss Lillibet smoothed her hair and cleared her throat. 'Not at all, Alice. I could never be disappointed in you. I shall just need something new to do, that's all.'

'I'm in the same boat myself, actually,' said James.

'*Moi aussi*,' said Mama. 'My job at the bank is finished. You must both come over to keep us company.'

'A fine idea,' said James. 'That dessert is so beautiful, it's a shame to cut it, Marie-Claire.'

And it was. The way Mama had done the chocolate bark, the *Bûche de Noël* looked exactly like the branch of a real tree. But it was so velvety and rich and delicious, they soon decided they didn't mind chopping it into logs and then twigs. Soon it had disappeared, and they all sat back, feeling a little ill, but Christmas ill, which wasn't bad at all.

'Oh my,' said Miss Lillibet, sitting back with her hands on her belly. 'That was phenomenal.'

'You'd better take a turn around the garden for some air, Miss Lillibet,' Alice said eagerly. 'You're looking a little pale. James will go with you in case you faint.'

'I'd be delighted,' said James, and as they pushed their chairs back, smiling, Alice wondered if her plan might be working before she'd even begun it. Were they falling in love? How did you tell?

'Mama, that was so scrumptious,' she said with a happy sigh.

'Papa Sir would have loved that *Bûche*,' said George. 'He was a fiend for chocolate, wasn't he, *Maman*?'

'*Oui*. Let us raise a glass to him. To Papa Sir!'

'To Papa Sir,' they said with lots of clinking.

'Dearie me, seems I'm just too late,' came a voice from the dusk – a Scottish voice. And there was Mrs McNair, Jilly's mother, in her Sunday-best clothes, a parcel under her arm, her lips thin and drawn together.

Alice hadn't seen Mrs McNair since the day she'd forbidden Alice to see Jilly ever again. But even though she'd heard from Jilly how much her mother had changed, Alice's chest felt tight with worry. Was Mrs McNair going to be awful and ruin their perfect Christmas dinner?

'*Joyeux Noël*, Madame McNair. Please, sit down,' said Mama, standing up to kiss her on both cheeks.

'Och. Aye, well . . .' said Mrs McNair, shifting uneasily on the spot.

'Is that a present you've brought?' asked Mabel.

'Aye – some Black Bun. It's meant for Hogmanay – Scottish New Year's Eve – as a sign of good things to come. But that's not why I'm here.'

'George, pour Mrs McNair a glass of water, *s'il vous-plait.*'

Mrs McNair sat down and started fidgeting with a napkin. She's nervous too, Alice realised, and let out a deep breath.

'There are things that've happened . . . things I'm not proud of,' said Mrs McNair. 'With my Douglas, as you know.'

'But that wasn't your fault – that was the war,' said Alice, and they all nodded. Alice was surprised by how good it felt to be kind to Mrs McNair. I'm forgiving her, she realised. And it isn't so tricky after all.

'Nice o' you to say, I'm sure, but there's things that came before that.' Mrs McNair was trembling now. What on earth was she going to say?

The laughter of James and Miss Lillibet floated up from somewhere quite far away – perhaps as far as the big elm tree, which would be a nice place to kiss, Alice thought. A romantic place.

But her imaginings were cut short as Mrs McNair cleared her throat noisily.

'It was . . . it was me who put the white feathers in the mail to your Teddy,' she said, all in a rush. 'It was me who baited him into goin' to war by calling him a coward.'

Alice felt her cheeks go hot and her insides turn cold.

Mabel gasped. 'You *didn't*!'

'So I've done somethin' to make amends,' Mrs McNair continued hastily. 'My husband's high up in the forces now, and he's arranged that

Teddy be allowed to come home on the next ship – instead o' my Hamish. Teddy'll be home in six weeks' time. It's not enough, I know. But it's something to show that I'm sorry.'

Alice felt a big hate pooling in her heart. She stood up and realised she was going to do something awful. She was going to slap Mrs McNair.

But then Mama was stroking Alice's forearm with her cool, long fingers. 'There is not one of us who 'as come through the war without regrets – not one,' she said. 'Me, I regret that often I was not 'ome – that my family was alone when they needed me. I regret that I did not protest when the Schultz brothers were taken away and put in that 'orrible camp on Rottnest Island. *Oui*, the war 'as brought with it many types of shame.

'But with this comes chances, *non*? Chances to do better. Forgiveness is what stops wars from beginning. And so I forgive you,

Nettie – *oui*. I do. I love my son, and 'e is safe. So with the thanks in my heart, I forgive you.'

Alice felt she had never heard Mama speak so beautifully, and her chest ached with admiration and her throat hurt with pride. If Mama can be so brave, perhaps I can be, too, thought Alice. She pulled herself up very straight, as if she were standing at the barre.

'Thank you, Mrs McNair,' she said, 'for letting Teddy take Hamish's place and come home. That was very kind.'

'Thank you,' murmured Mabel and George and Little together.

'Oh, no, thank *you*. I dunnae deserve your forgiveness – least, not so swiftly,' said Mrs McNair.

At that moment, Miss Lillibet and James came back around the corner, arm in arm.

'An addition to our party!' said James warmly. 'Merry Christmas, madam. I'm

James Busby-Wilks. Do you like to dance? I'm suddenly in the mood.'

After they had put out their shoes in front of the fireplace for *Père Noël* to fill with gifts, Alice lay in bed, thinking about what Mama had said about everyone having regrets from the war. Is my big regret that I gave up dancing? Should I start again? she wondered. Now the war is over and Teddy will be home and Miss Lillibet is free, why shouldn't I do nice things?

But the idea filled her with dread, and suddenly Alice knew the reason she hadn't started again; she realised she'd known it all along. I'm worried I won't be any good, she thought. I'm afraid that I won't be perfect. I'm just scared.

5

TEDDY COMES HOME

THE shock of what Mrs McNair had revealed at Christmas was quickly overtaken by the realisation that Teddy would soon be with them. And so for the next few weeks they worked harder than ever in the hot January sunshine to tidy the garden, and dust and air his room, and shine his shoes, and make the whole house pretty.

Without anyone asking, James came each day to help, sometimes even before breakfast, stopping only to go down to the river for a swim at lunchtime. Even with one hand, he was fast and strong, and he left a frothy churn of water behind him that made Pudding very excited when they went down to watch.

They all loved James, each for a different reason. He was kind and gentle, like Teddy, and a great tease, like Papa Sir. And just like Papa Sir – like all of them – he loved silly nicknames. For no particular reason he called Alice 'Birdy' and Mabel 'Ducks' and Pudding 'My Bonnie Robin'. And when he was with them, it was easy to forget there was anything bad in the world.

But there was someone that Alice wanted to love him the best – to love him enough to move to a fruit farm. Luckily, that someone was also at the house a lot, chatting with Mama and helping to paint the high-up bit of the front gate because she was so tall.

Each time they smiled at each other across the table, Alice jiggled her feet with excitement. James hasn't come home for nothing, she thought with happy relief. He's come home for love, after all.

The big day finally came, and it started with crepes and fresh butter, which Mama had whipped herself. When Alice came down to breakfast, she found James at the table, tucking in next to George. To Alice's surprise, so was Miss Lillibet.

'Miss Lillibet! What's brought you here so early?'

And to Alice's delight, Miss Lillibet blushed, the kind of pink, pretty flush that could only mean one thing. James gazed at her across the table, almost knocking over the little pitcher of Honey's milk.

'Well . . . it's a special day,' she said. 'I can't stay till the afternoon, but I wanted to – to help you make things nice for Teddy.'

'Oh good, because there's still lots to do. Would you mind hanging up the streamers around the front door?' said Alice. 'And James, if it's not too much trouble, could you please mow the tennis court and paint on the white lines this morning? I want to play against Teddy as soon as he's back so he can see how much my serve has improved. Mabel, could you go and double-check that his paint brushes are all lined up? Now Pudding, what are you going to say when Teddy arrives? Remember what we practised?'

Pudding nodded.

'Little, you're on baking duty of course. And George, have you finished the banner?'

'It's drying on the back verandah.'

They had spent a lot of time arguing over what the banner should say. George thought it should be in Latin, while Mabel had been determined to rhyme 'Hip Hip Hooray' with 'You've lived to fight another day'. In the end they had settled on something simple: *Teddy, We're SO Glad You're Home.*

By lunchtime, James was still finishing up the lines on the tennis court, but everything else was exactly how Alice wanted it.

Eventually, Miss Lillibet had to leave, but she made Alice promise to give Teddy her special love. The table was set for tea and groaning with food.

Only Mama wasn't there – she'd ducked over to the McNairs' house to invite them all to join the tea later. Since Christmas, she had tried very hard to be friendly, and Mrs McNair had tried even harder in return.

Then came the merry *parp* of a horn, and they all rushed out to stand under the banner.

'Teddy,' Alice cried as Uncle Bear edged Rough-and-Tumble up the driveway. They all waved madly, bouncing on their toes with the thrill of seeing Teddy again. He looked just the same as ever.

Actually . . . that wasn't right.

In his uniform, he looked older and even more handsome. His chest was broader, his arms thicker. His hair was cut so short that you couldn't see the curls. Alice couldn't look away from his face; it made her so happy.

But as they pulled up to the verandah, Teddy wasn't looking at her. He sat in Rough-and-Tumble's sidecar, peering out at the garden. 'Who's that on the tennis court?' he said, his voice sharp and frosty.

'Oh, that's just James – you'll like him.' Alice leaned over the sidecar and threw her arms around him. 'Teddy, you're back! It's so good to see you. And we've all sorts of things to show you tomorrow. First I thought we'd have a game of tennis. Then after breakfast we'll pack a picnic with your paints and go down to the river. There's something you need to see down there,' she said, thinking of Papa Sir's boat, which Uncle Bear had finished for them. 'You won't believe it, it's too wonderful. Then –'

'Can't I just do as I like?' Teddy said sharply, his arms stiff at his sides. 'I had enough people ordering me about in the army.'

Alice stepped back. 'Of course,' she said, trying to keep her voice steady. 'Those were just suggestions. You must be very tired. We'll carry in your things.'

He climbed out of the sidecar and walked past them all and up the front steps, not stopping to look at the banner and the streamers.

Pudding stepped forward and took a deep breath. But Teddy didn't even glance at her. He kept walking through the hall and up the stairs to his bedroom.

'Join us for your welcome tea when you're ready,' Alice called after him as his bedroom door clicked shut.

Alice wanted to run, then, and leap back onto her bed and tuck her head under her pillow to weep her disappointment away. But as she turned to go, she saw the others standing frozen in the hallway, waiting for her to say or do something to make it right.

'Who feels like something to eat?' she asked briskly. 'Mama's made frangipane tarts. She'll be back any moment, and Teddy will come down when he's had a little rest, I'm sure. He's come a long way, hasn't he.'

But Teddy didn't come down for tea, or for supper, and when Alice tapped on his door with some cocoa as the sun set, there was no answer at all.

It took days for Teddy to leave his room, and when he did, he would only come down in small patches to sit on the verandah, scowling at James as he worked in the orchard — scowling at them all.

At first, Alice tried to cheer him up. She

told him about the Apple Blossom Fair and Uncle Bear finishing off Papa Sir's boat. She told him about Lionel Logue and Pudding learning to talk. She read to him from the newspaper about how Spanish flu had reached Australia, how in Victoria and New South Wales they'd closed the schools and theatres, and people had to wear masks when they went outside, even to church.

But Teddy didn't seem to care. Most of the time, he didn't even seem to be listening.

'Would you like us to put on a play for you? What about the one with the Scottish bears?' Alice asked one afternoon, desperately trying to fill Teddy's prickly silence.

'Wasn't the war punishment enough?' said Teddy, glowering at Pudding, who was driving Tatty's cart around the neat, mown lawn.

'Hi!' she called. 'Hi, Teddy, hi! See my nice goat?'

But though Alice was sure that was the first

time Pudding had ever said his name, Teddy acted like he hadn't heard.

Alice tried to tell herself that it wasn't her job to care so much, that it wasn't her fault that the littlies were all frightened of Teddy now – that she was, too. 'Well, what about a swim? I bet you're even faster now. You could start training for the Swim-Through.'

Teddy gritted his teeth. 'Stop your goddamn meddling and *leave me the hell alone.*' He jumped up and grabbed a handful of gravel from the big stone vase by the door. Then he hurled the stones at Tatty, and they flew through the air like sharp little bullets, hitting the lawn just a few feet from Pudding's shocked, pudgy face.

To Alice's astonishment, the next morning Teddy came down before they'd finished breakfast and he sat in his normal seat at the table. Alice felt her insides swoop, as if she'd just taken off in a hot air balloon. Everything'll go back to how it was, she told herself. It might take time, but it will – you'll see.

'It's a lovely day outside. Perhaps you could do some painting today,' she said to Teddy as she spread jam on her toast. 'Mabel cleaned all your brushes specially.'

Teddy scoffed. 'As if I paint anymore.

Pointless waste of time. You can throw all that stuff away. I won't be using it.'

'Oh,' said Alice sadly, thinking suddenly of her ballet shoes, stuffed at the back of her closet.

'But why?' asked Mabel. 'What's that got to do with the war?'

'Everything,' said Teddy, and gritted his teeth again.

'Tell us about the war then – you haven't said a word about it,' said Mabel impatiently.

'I'm not sure he wants to,' said Alice quickly. She turned to Teddy. 'We know from your letters that it wasn't very nice.'

'Still, it must have been quite an adventure, mustn't it?' said Mabel. 'Going all the way across the world, and seeing France and things? That would have been exciting. And you survived! That was jolly lucky.'

Teddy looked at Mabel with dead, flat eyes. And then his chest started heaving, and as he put his hand to his throat, he started coughing – the most horrible cough that Alice had ever heard. On and on he rasped in hoarse, gasping moans, his eyes streaming. Pudding climbed off her seat and up onto Alice's lap. Mabel leapt up to pat him on the back, but he shoved her aside with so much force that she stumbled.

'You were gassed,' said George solemnly when Teddy had finished.

'What do you mean?' asked Alice.

'I've read about it. The Germans used mustard gas – the British, too, eventually. As a weapon. It caused soldiers to . . . to . . .'

'Go blind,' Teddy croaked, and swallowed to clear his throat. 'Burst out in vile sores. Hack and cough until their lungs bled. Die writhing in agony. That sort of thing. I suppose that was quite exciting, Mabel.' He swallowed. 'That, and seeing rats chewing dead men's ears off. And watching the skin on my feet peeling off in putrid layers because I had trench foot from the mud that came up to my —'

'Stop,' cried Little, putting her hands over her ears. 'Stop stop stop.'

Alice had never seen Mabel look so terrified. She hugged Pudding tight, not knowing what to say.

'I'm sorry, Teddy,' Mabel whispered. 'I'm so sorry.'

But Teddy just stared at her. 'You're right. It's jolly lucky I survived so I can lie awake thinking about that,' he said, standing up.

Alice looked at the others, and saw that Little had crawled under the table. She saw that George had tears in his eyes.

Then a storm was building inside her, and suddenly she jumped up and ran after Teddy, and grabbed his forearm so sharply that she felt the pull of his shoulder. He turned around in surprise.

'How *dare* you be so horrible to Mabel,' she

shouted. 'And how dare you mope around all day and scare the children. I know you've seen awful things and I'm sure it was very hard. But so has James, and he's still nice to us. And even though he only has one hand, he helps us every single day, and he goes and swims in the river. All you've got is a bit of a cough and you do nothing but sit around. I don't even know why you bothered coming back, Teddy. You're selfish and horrible and I wish you were *dead*.'

With all the strength she'd built improving the serve that Teddy refused to watch, she flung his arm back at his chest and marched off to find Jilly.

'But Jilly, you didn't see me – I was *awful*. I said the most horrible things. As soon as they came out of my mouth, I felt sick to my stomach,' Alice confided as they paddled George's canoe out to lower his kerosene tins, which they'd baited to catch crabs. Crabs were Teddy's favourite food.

'It sounds to me like he might have deserved them,' said Jilly.

'It's not his fault he's like this – it's the war. Same as with Douglas.' Alice tested the knots on her rope. 'But I don't care if I have to try a million different things, I'm going to cheer him up. He can't stay miserable forever. Now, what usually cheers people up?'

'Food,' said Jilly. 'So the crabs are a start. What about a picnic at the river?'

'Well, he still hasn't seen Papa Sir's boat. I'm sure James would take us out on it if we asked him. But can you think of anything else – anything more spectacular? What's the most . . . the most *breathtaking* thing you can imagine?'

Jilly leaned over and dangled her fingers into the water, tapping them on the surface to form rings. 'You know, you could dance for him, Alice.'

'I *told* you, Jilly. I'm not –'

'Not even for Teddy? He loved seeing you dance. Which reminds me. Ballet auditions for the peacetime concert are next week – are you going to come? We're doing *The Fairy Snow Queen*. Remember how much Teddy loved it when you were in that?'

Alice looked across at Jilly, feeling her heart slam against her ribs. This was the first she had heard of a peacetime concert. They'd danced *The Fairy Snow Queen* two years ago, and Alice had been the star part – the beautiful queen who danced to the end of the world to break the spell that had frozen her wings. Alice felt that she'd practised so hard and loved it so much, she hadn't just danced the part – she *was* the Fairy Snow Queen. Or at least, she had been.

'I'm only telling you this because you're

my best friend,' Jilly said. 'But the reason you won't come back to class, Alice Alexander, is because you're scared. You're scared that you won't be as good as you were before. And it's fine to be scared. But it's not fine to do nothing about it.'

Though Alice had thought the very same thing, it hurt to hear it. 'It's not very nice, Jilly,' she said in a tight voice, 'to call me a coward.'

'You're only a coward if you act like a coward,' said Jilly calmly as they rowed back towards the shore. 'You're the best dancer anyone around here has seen. If I were even half as talented as you, I'd be dancing every chance I had. And so would any of the other girls. So think about that next time you're feeling sorry for yourself because you can't let yourself try. It's a choice, Alice. And it's yours.'

7

SOMETHING VERY UNEXPECTED

ON the last day of the holidays, as Alice started to pull everyone's school pinafores out of the cupboard, she made a long list in her mind of all the things she needed to do: make sure everyone had clean socks and the girls had ribbons, fetch their shoes for polishing and their satchels for clearing out. Hopefully Mabel wouldn't have left any putrid apples in her bag, like last year. Alice wished she'd thought to check about the clean clothes earlier, for now she'd have to light the copper if she wanted to wash and wring them out. It felt good to think about practical things; it helped her push her guilt away. For Teddy hadn't come out of his room since she'd said those hateful words.

Mama left food outside his door at night, but each morning when Alice went to collect the tray, it was untouched. The only sound that came from his room was the occasional hoarse gasps of that awful cough. If he wastes away, it will be all my fault, Alice told herself fiercely. And Jilly's right – I'm too much of a coward to dance, even if it would save Teddy's life.

But when Mama found her hunting for pairs of bloomers, she shooed Alice away.

'*Tiens!* Do not be spending your last day of freedom doing boring chores. I shall wash for the children. Go out – enjoy the sun.'

'Are you sure, Mama? I've always done it before – I don't mind.'

Mama looked at her with worry and tenderness, all mixed together, and took

Little's bloomers from her hands. 'I am afraid that all the time I was working, I stopped you being a leetle girl.'

'I'm not little, and I liked it, Mama.' She paused. 'And I think I was good at it,' she said. 'But if you're sure, I'll go and see Jilly.'

'*Absolument.*'

'Mama?' said Alice. 'I know you liked working, but it's so nice having you home.'

Mama smiled fondly at Alice. 'I 'ad thought that without my job, I would be miserable. But I love being with my family. And I 'ave loved cooking for you, and caring for you. It 'as been too long since I did this properly. You carried everyone through the war, *ma petite*. And now, let go of us all and be free.'

Alice kissed Mama on the cheek, feeling as if something heavier than the world had been lifted from her back. Mama was right – she had done it. The war really was over, and though Papa Sir was gone forever, Alice had kept the rest of them safe. She felt as if she'd managed to shield a tiny candle from a roaring wind by cupping it carefully in her hand.

Alice sprinted up to her bedroom, lifted the mattress and snatched the big cream envelope that lay there, shoving it into the pocket of her dress. It was the letter from her audition with Edouard Espinosa; Alice had almost forgotten about it, she'd kept it secret so long. But now she'd show Jilly, and tell her that she'd made up her mind. I'll dance the Fairy Snow Queen, and Teddy will be happy and Miss Lillibet will be proud. And Jilly won't think I'm a coward any longer, she thought as she ran back downstairs and through the kitchen and raced across the lawn to Jilly's house. Just this morning I was so gloomy, and now I truly believe I could fly.

Jilly's mother opened the door and smiled warmly at Alice. 'Come in, dearie,' she said. 'They're up in the nursery.'

Alice took the stairs two at a time. As she ran up the hallway, she heard some very familiar music coming from the nursery.

'Jilly? Guess what!' she called as she burst in, fishing out the envelope to show her friend. 'I'm going to audition!'

There stood Jilly in her dance tunic and her ballet shoes, and next to her was Miss Lillibet, shaping Jilly's arms into a fifth position.

And then Alice realised: the music on the gramophone was the opening solo dance of the Fairy Snow Queen.

'You're too late,' said Jilly, a look of mortification on her freckly face. 'The auditions were yesterday and I didn't want to tell you yet but . . . but *I'm* the Fairy Snow Queen. I auditioned and I got the part and Miss Lillibet is helping me learn it because there isn't much time before the concert.'

'Dear Alice, Jilly told me you'd made up your mind,' said Miss Lillibet guiltily.

As Alice stood looking at her two favourite people, she felt as if the roof of her world was crumbling down. She wanted to say something, but her throat hurt more than when she'd had tonsillitis and Papa Sir had made her ice-cream that was really just sweet dribbles of cold milk.

'I'll give it up,' said Jilly desperately. 'I'll tell Miss Josephine that I won't do it – I'll go and tell her this afternoon.'

But as Alice tried to swallow down her sadness, she thought of all the times she'd been the star, and how proud Jilly had been, and excited. 'You'll do no such thing, Jilly McNair,' she said. 'You earned the part fair and square, and you'll be wonderful. Miss Lillibet is the best teacher in the world.'

Relief flooded colour back into Jilly's face, and Miss Lillibet smiled at Alice. But as Alice turned to go, her eyes filled with tears.

'Oh – Alice?' Jilly called after her.

'Yes?' croaked Alice, not turning around.

'Do you still have the tiara from the last concert? Miss Lillibet thought I should practise in it. Could you bring it over?'

Alice nodded and shoved the big cream envelope back into her pocket as she ran out the door.

Slumping along by the river, Alice's head throbbed. Don't you *dare* be jealous, she told herself. It's your own stupid fault.

As she passed the Scotch College boatshed, she saw James climbing out of the water to lie on the warm wooden slats of the jetty. She wandered over and lay down beside him. 'Hi James. Did you have a good swim?'

'My best time yet. Should be right for the Swim-Through in a few weeks' time.' James propped himself up on his elbow to look into Alice's face. 'You're glum, Birdy. What's shaking?'

Alice looked out at the river, which was so still and peaceful, it seemed to be mocking her. 'I . . . I might be a murderer soon,' she said, and then felt silly for being so dramatic.

But James didn't laugh or tease. 'Hmm. Prison's tough. Why don't you give me the background, and we'll try to avoid it?'

Alice turned over onto her stomach and squinted through the gaps in the jetty to watch the water lap and sparkle below.

'Have you ever felt like you were once very good at something . . . and then you had to watch someone overtake you – someone who you knew, in your heart, wasn't as good?'

James was silent, and as Alice turned to look at him, she saw he was holding out his arm to her – the one without the hand. His stump looked raw and sore. She remembered how he had once played cricket; the wishful look on his face when he'd told her. Alice realised that if anyone understood what it felt like to lose a part of yourself, it was James.

'Mine sounds so silly, compared to you losing your hand. I can't even say it.'

'You could never sound silly to me, Birdy.'

Alice took a deep breath. 'Jilly's going to dance the role of the Fairy Snow Queen at the peacetime concert. And that's my favourite part in the world. I danced it two years ago, and it was the first time I believed that I might one day be a real dancer. I feel so mean, but I'm not sure how I'll be able to go and watch her, even though she's always watched me be the star. Because before I knew you, James, and before Teddy left, and before the war, I used to be a ballerina.' The word sounded so pretty, so simple.

'Everything felt easy then, and I didn't have any worries – not hardly one.' Alice watched as one of her tears slid down her nose and plopped through a gap in the jetty. She waited for it to hit the water, but it was too small to make a splash. 'But now I'm too frightened to dance. And everything's a jumbled mess because of me.' She closed her eyes.

'Bird? I need you to look at me,' James said, and his voice was so tender that Alice turned and looked.

'You don't have to make everything all right for everyone. Sometimes there are things that can't be changed or mended.'

Alice thought about it for a moment. 'But I'm the fixer – I'm the glue that holds us together. Teddy told me, before he left.'

James shook his head. 'That's what you do. Just as ballet was something you did, and you might do again, if you choose. But it's not who you are. You're Alice Alexander of Peppermint Grove,' he said, 'and nothing you fix or start or stop can change that. Whatever you do, you're already perfect. Just as you are.'

Alice of Peppermint Grove. It sounds nice,

Alice thought, through her tears. It sounds like someone I hope I might be one day.

'As for the concert,' James continued, 'give yourself some time to decide. You might just surprise yourself and go along after all. But either way, I won't think any less of you, and I doubt Jilly will either.'

Then Alice leaned forward and squeezed James tight. He hugged her back, and his arms around her felt warm and safe.

'You hug just like my father,' she said in wonder. 'James,' she said as they let each other go. 'I'm glad that you came to us – that Mabel wasn't Arabella.'

'Alice Alexander, I wouldn't trade you for all the Arabellas in the world.'

As Alice walked up through the orchard toward home, she could see Teddy sitting on the verandah, watching her – or perhaps he wasn't at all. But it didn't matter, because he was there, not dead in his room or dead on a field in France. He looked so small and alone in his rocking chair that Alice's heart panged.

'Teddy,' she said when she reached him, 'I'm sorry for what I said. I'm sorry that I don't know how to cheer you up.'

'And I'm sorry,' said Teddy, 'that I'm not James.'

She spun around, and Teddy was looking right at her with his Papa Sir eyes.

'I don't want you to be James,' she said. 'I just want you here. And you are.'

He looked back out at the garden. 'I can't go around pretending I'm the same chap I was before I left,' he said.

Alice had never known so deeply that Teddy was her brother; that there were things they shared that didn't have words or names. 'I don't want you to pretend,' she said quietly. 'Promise me you never will.'

8

THE SWIM-THROUGH

BACK at school, it seemed all anyone could talk about was the Big Weekend in March: the Swim-Through which would be on a Saturday morning, followed by the peacetime concert on Sunday afternoon.

At elevenses, Podger started taking bets about who would win the swim. Alice and Jilly stood with a group of girls on the side of the asphalt, watching them line up and wager their pocket money or their marbles.

'Oi, Alice,' called Septimus Burt. 'Is your brother racing? I reckon he's in with a shot.

Podger, take my fiver for Teddy Alexander to win.'

'Don't – he's not racing,' Alice said. 'He's . . . he's just not.'

'Perhaps they should start taking a bet about whether the whole thing will go ahead,' said Ada.

'What do you mean?' Alice asked, thinking of how hard James had been training.

'Well, I've heard that in the eastern states people aren't allowed to meet in big groups because of the Spanish flu. They don't want it to spread, so the theatres are closed and everything – no public gatherings at all. I expect that will happen here soon.'

'Oh dear,' said Jilly to Alice. 'What if it does and we can't do the peacetime concert?'

'That would be terrible,' Alice replied untruthfully. It was a wicked thing to wish that the concert would be called off, but she did it anyway, trying to push away the memory of Jilly's sparkling face when Alice had given her the tiara that morning.

'It's silly to be so excited, I know,' Jilly had said apologetically. 'But I've never been the star of anything before. Even in the Christmas nativity, I was always just the innkeeper's daughter.'

'It's not silly at all,' said Alice firmly. 'It's a big part. And you'll be wonderful.'

The Swim-Through wasn't cancelled, and the early March sun was high in the sky as Alice and her family arrived at Mosman Bay a few weeks' later to watch it. The foreshore was a field of bobbing hats: square straw boaters; white, puffy meringue hats that tied under ladies' chins; little bonnets that shaded chubby babies in their big-wheeled prams. Mama had Pudding on her shoulders, and George had Little on his back.

'Come on, Alice,' said Mabel, 'I'll get us to the front.' She set off through the crowd with her elbows stuck out and weaved her way right to the front, where the crowd had gathered round the finishing line in a half moon. They found Miss Lillibet there and slipped in beside her as Ginger, the policeman, stood atop a ladder on the jetty, pistol in one hand and a megaphone in the other.

'All competitors are to follow the course out to the buoy, around the Point Walter spit post, to Keane's Point, and back to the jetty. TAKE your *marrrrrks*, GET set . . . GO!'

When the starting gun went off, the crowd roared and the water bubbled like bath foam, and the fins of bent elbows popped up through the choppy waves.

'Busby-Wilks is leading them out,' called a man with binoculars and a twirly moustache. 'Beautiful stroke style.'

'But can he stay the distance? My money's on Rolf Nyman,' said Ford, the stationmaster.

'I wonder what's on their minds while

they're out there,' mused Miss Lillibet. 'What do you think, Alice?'

'I bet James is picturing you, Miss Lillibet,' said Alice, grinning. 'And that's what's making him go so fast.' Alice looked up at her with delight. But Miss Lillibet looked as if she would be ill, right there on the foreshore. Her face had turned green with horror or maybe fright – Alice couldn't tell which.

But she didn't have the chance to ask, because suddenly the crowd was jostling and parting, and someone was yelling, 'Make way! Make way! Quickly – *please*.'

Alice didn't have to turn around to know that voice. And as Teddy pushed past her in his swimming trunks, Alice felt as if she were in a happy dream.

'Catch 'em, Teddy!' yelled Septimus Burt.

And as Teddy sprinted to the water and threw himself into the shallows, the whole crowd joined in.

'Te-ddy, Te-ddy, Te-ddy,' they roared as his legs churned and his arms whirled like propellers.

'Te-ddy, *Te-ddy*,' screamed Alice and Mabel as they clutched each other and jumped up and down.

With each stroke, Teddy drew closer to the roiling pack of swimmers. It seemed to Alice as if they were almost treading water, they were so slow in comparison. As he rounded the buoy, he caught up to one, and then another. Alice thought she would go deaf, Mabel's shrieks were so loud.

The stretch from the buoy to the Point Walter spit was the longest. What if he tires? Alice thought desperately.

But Teddy didn't tire. He pulled away from everyone, stroking in the smooth, strong rhythm that Alice knew was his alone. He's going to win, she thought incredulously as he reached the spit and turned for the final sprint to the jetty, where the crowd, wild with delight, willed him on as one. He's going to win, and he'll be happy again. Alice felt giddy with relief, and reached out for Miss Lillibet's hand only to find that Miss Lillibet was wiping her eyes and weeping.

But as he neared the finish line, Teddy stopped swimming; his arms stopped whirling, his head went under.

The crowd buzzed with confusion, and then went quiet.

'What's he playing at? Duck-diving for pennies?' called Ford.

Nobody laughed, because when Teddy surfaced, an awful sound rang out across the water — a sound that was so familiar to Alice by now. It was the hoarse, gasping moan of Teddy's gas cough.

And then there was just the silence of him sinking, down, down, down.

9

HOPE AND THE WIDE, BRIGHT SKY

IT was James who pulled Teddy out of the river. He would have won the Swim-Through if he hadn't stopped to wrench Teddy, limp and grey, from the water, and dragged his body through the shallows. It didn't take long before Teddy spluttered and opened his eyes, but those awful seconds would be with Alice forever, she was sure.

She thought about them the next afternoon as she lay on her bed, listening to the excited chatter of everyone leaving for the peacetime concert without her.

James had knocked on her door earlier, but she hadn't answered, and now she regretted it. Yesterday had been such a blur that she hadn't even really thanked him properly.

As the grandfather clock boomed, Alice felt sick and hollow. I can't stand to go and watch Jilly, but I can't stand to be by myself either, she thought crossly. I'm horrible.

When the last chime had died away, she went in search of Teddy. Eventually she found him in the greenhouse, wrapped up in a blanket.

He turned as she let herself in, and looked at her in surprise. 'Why aren't you at the concert?' he asked. 'Isn't it Jilly's big day?'

She sighed. 'I didn't go. I couldn't watch because it used to be me.' Alice walked over to the clotheshorse that was once her ballet barre and rested her hands on it, looking out at the Sunday sailboats on the river below. 'Do you think I'm disgusting?' she asked Teddy.

Teddy went to answer, but he broke out

in his hacking, raspy cough, which bounced off the glass walls and made Alice's ears ring painfully.

'You're not disgusting,' Teddy said when he had recovered. 'But it's just not like you.'

'I don't feel like me,' she said. 'Everything feels wrong.'

'What would make it right?' asked Teddy.

I can stand at the back, Alice thought as she ran through the quiet, green streets of Peppermint Grove, and hopefully no one will notice me, and I'll still be able to congratulate Jilly afterwards. But as she got closer to St Columba's, the church hall was ringing not with music but with loud chatting. She slipped in the back door to find that the dancing hadn't started yet. People were fidgeting and some were getting up – it looked as though they were leaving.

'Alice! I was about to run home to get you,' said Mabel urgently, appearing by her side. 'Jilly needs you! This *second*.'

She yanked Alice out the door and round the back of the hall, where the little church kitchen had been turned into a dressing room. Jilly was sitting with her ankle propped up on a bucket and a bandage round it, her cheeks wet, her nose dripping, and the Fairy Snow Queen's silk dress on her lap.

Alice gasped. 'Jilly – your big part! Oh *no*! I'm so sorry. What are you going to . . .' She trailed off as Jilly held out the beautiful costume to her. Suddenly she realised what her best friend was asking her to do.

'I can't, I can't, I can't,' Alice said shaking her head frantically. 'I haven't danced in months – I wouldn't be any good.'

'You're the only one who knows the part. *Please* – if you don't do it, the show can't happen, and we've been practising so hard.'

Alice walked around and around in tight circles, her mind a storm of panic. She looked over at poor Jilly, whose eyes were so full of tears that Alice had to turn away to stop herself from crying, too. Jilly just wanted to be the star – just once, thought Alice. I shouldn't have minded that it wasn't me. And I shouldn't mind that I haven't practised – I'll remember the steps when I hear the music.

But Alice knew that dancing wasn't as simple as that for her. I won't be as good – I won't be able to jump as high or stretch as far, and my point won't be sharp, and my dancing won't be beautiful, she thought wildly. I'll get puffed. I might trip. And people will say that I'm not good enough to be a real dancer.

'But I don't even want to be a dancer anymore,' she cried, not realising she was speaking aloud.

'Is that so?' said a familiar voice.

'James,' said Alice, spinning around, her

eyes prickling. 'I'm supposed to – they want me – Jilly –'

James held up his hand. 'I've heard, Alice. Come, now, and take a walk with me. Jilly, you won't mind, will you? We'll be back in a few minutes.'

'The audience will have left by then,' said Mabel. 'A few people already have.'

'Sing for them, Ducks. Distract them. Get George up there if you have to,' said James, putting his arm around Alice's shoulder and leading her out the side of the hall and over to the bench by the wishing well.

'James, please don't make me,' said Alice desperately as they sat down. 'I won't be any good. I'll be sick all over the stage.' Her fingers were twisted so tightly together that her knuckles bulged like white marbles.

James reached into his satchel and pulled out an oblong parcel, wrapped in brown paper, and handed it to Alice. 'Then you'll be wanting this. I brought it to give to you after the performance – if you came, which I suspected you would. Open it, Alice.'

Alice tore the paper to reveal a book, pale green with a twirling black-and-white pattern pressed into its cover.

She opened it, and she felt a beautiful warmth unfurl in her chest. '*Hope and the Wide, Bright Sky* by Babington Wilder: First Edition,' Alice read from the title page. And there was a message, written in the most elegant handwriting. '*With hope and love to the reader of this book, from your friend and companion, Babington Wilder.*'

Alice looked at James in wonder. 'For me?'

James smiled. 'For you, Bird. To keep for always. I underlined a passage – where the corner of the page is turned over. I hope you don't mind, but I read it and thought of you.' He stood up and kissed the top of her head. 'Whatever you decide, I'll be waiting,' he said, and walked back inside.

Leafing through the book to the page with the turned-down corner, Alice flipped past sentences she had read over and over – that she'd had read to her by Teddy before she was old enough to know them for herself. So when she got to the underlined words, it was Teddy's voice that she heard, clear and calm and steady. It was the voice he'd had before the war, before he was cold and gruff.

Said Hope to the Boy on the edge of the sill, 'How lucky you are to be able to fly.'

Said the Boy with a frown, 'I'd cut off my wings if I could, but they'd only grow back.'

'Don't you like to fly?' asked Hope in surprise. 'Doesn't it make you feel free?'

'It frightens me,' scowled the Boy. 'How do I know that my wings will support me?'

Hope laughed prettily. 'But that's what they're for, Boy.'

Said the Boy, 'Do not laugh. How would you

*like to feel you're a coward? Always to tremble and
never be brave?'*

'Why, if that's the case, you're brave every day,'
Hope said, and tossed her golden hair. *'To be all that
you are in spite of your fear, why, that's bravery.
And to use what you have even when you might fail,
now that's courage. Does that cheer you, Boy?'*

*The Boy held out his feather to her, and she took
it and put it behind her ear. He tiptoed to the edge
of the ledge, and Reader, he paused — and he flew.*

Alice closed the book and stood up. She walked
slowly back to the hall, and there was Mama
standing outside the doorway, bending over
and fanning herself.

'Mama,' Alice said. 'I'm going to dance. I'm
going to be the Fairy Snow Queen.'

'What are they laughing at?' Alice asked Mabel
as she tied on Jilly's ballet shoes, which were

luckily only the tiniest bit too big.

'It's George, reading his opus. You won't believe it, but he's bringing the house down.'

Alice couldn't believe it, but as she twisted up her hair and topped it with the glittering tiara, the hall rocked with stamping feet, and the air rung with whistles. Oh George, she thought. They love you! I'm so sorry I called you a bore.

When he came off the stage, Alice was waiting in the wings to grab him and plant a big kiss on his face.

He frowned and wiped it away. 'Urgh, what was that for?'

'I didn't take your opus very seriously, and I should have,' said Alice. 'I'm so sorry. You must be a wonderful writer. People would have left if it wasn't for your opus.'

'That's all right, Alice. Genius is rarely understood.'

'You're a dark horse, writing something funny. I thought you were working on a tragedy.'

George looked down and shook his head. 'It was,' he said. 'But people couldn't stop laughing. I admit that I'm rather perplexed by the whole affair.'

'I wouldn't worry,' said Alice seriously, though she badly wanted to smile. 'As you say, genius is rarely understood.'

Then someone put on the gramophone and a light shone down the middle of the stage, and Alice ran to it. She pointed her foot behind her and brought her arms to third position, soft and supple and strong. The curtains opened, the music swelled, the audience applauded.

And Alice knew with everything in her that this was what she wanted to do for the rest of her life.

When the Fairy Snow Queen curtseyed for the final time, a tiny girl brought out a bouquet of white roses for Alice. Then the audience were on their feet shouting 'Bravo! Bravo!' and Alice had to wipe her eyes.

She glanced down and saw dear, poor Jilly crying, and Mama and Little, too. Mabel was standing on her chair, one hand on James's shoulder. And at the back of the hall she thought she might have seen Teddy, but perhaps it was only wishing. She ran off the stage and on again, but the clapping wouldn't stop; it just thundered around her like rain on the roof. As she looked out at the crowd, for the first time in such a long time the world felt light and free.

She didn't see the moment when Mama fell to the ground. She only realised it had happened when people started to crowd around in a tight little huddle that Alice had to burst through once she'd leapt from the stage to another wave of applause.

'What's wrong?' she cried. 'Mama?'

'She's burning up – she's got a fever,' said

George, putting his hand to Mama's smooth forehead. 'I'm sure of it. And look – she's got a rash on her neck. Mama?' he said loudly.

But Mama didn't respond.

'I'm calling for the doctor,' said James.

'Take Pudding and Little away, will you, James?' George asked as he tried to shake Mama a little more roughly.

Alice knelt down beside her and brushed her cheek against Mama's lips, not caring that the Fairy Snow Queen's tiara clattered to the ground. 'She's breathing – though why's it so rattly? Mama, can you hear me?' she asked desperately, and stroked Mama's beautiful hair. She felt something wet, and pulled her hand away. 'What's this sticky stuff around her ears, George?'

They looked down at Alice's hand, which was covered in something dark and streaky, and then back up at each other.

It was blood.

HOW I BECAME AN AUSTRALIAN GIRL

by Davina Bell

Like most Australian girls, my heritage
is a patchwork of pieces from many
places, stitched together by chance and
love. My parents met on the ski slopes
in Italy. Dad is Australian, but his
ancestors include a pair of Italian
apothecaries and an Irish minister,
and he grew up in Singapore. My mother,
who's English, went to a boarding school
called Battle Abbey and was a nurse in
a tiny African country called Lesotho,
where she lived in a mud hut with a
thatched roof.

I grew up in Perth, and on very hot days
when I couldn't play outside, I'd sit
and spin a globe for hours, waiting for
the afternoon sea breeze and picturing
life in those faraway places with their
strange lovely names. Perhaps all that
imagining is what led me to be a writer.

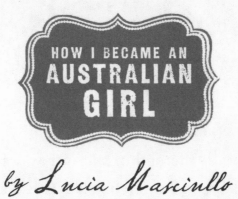

HOW I BECAME AN AUSTRALIAN GIRL

by Lucia Masciullo

I was born and grew up in Italy, a beautiful country to visit, but also a difficult country to live in for new generations.

In 2006, I packed up my suitcase and I left Italy with the man I love. We bet on Australia. I didn't know much about Australia before coming – I was just looking for new opportunities, I guess.

And I liked it right from the beginning! Australian people are resourceful, open-minded and always with a smile on their faces. I think all Australians keep in their blood a bit of the pioneer heritage, regardless of their own birthplace.

Here I began a new life and now I'm doing what I always dreamed of: I illustrate stories. Here is the place where I'd like to live and to grow up my children, in a country that doesn't fear the future.

Alice's Time

THOUGH the end of the war was a time for celebration and relief, it was also a sad time for many people, tinged with grief and worry.

For families who had lost their fathers and sons and brothers, it was a time of mourning and of accepting that they would never see their loved ones again.

Most soldiers had left feeling optimistic and brave about fighting, but had seen so many horrible things that they returned changed, feeling that war was awful and that the world was a terrible place. More than half were injured, and often this meant that they couldn't return to their old jobs. The government tried to help with pensions and land to farm in the country, but most of the time this was barely enough to support families, and many children had to go out to work.

A lot of soldiers had shell shock, which was an illness caused by the trauma of fighting. Many had painful wounds, shrapnel still inside their bodies, or pain where their arms and legs used to be. They had nightmares about the fighting, and some were so disturbed that they ended up in asylums. Because mustard gas had been used in the war as a weapon, many who had inhaled it by accident had scarred lungs that made it difficult to breathe or gave them coughs and chest infections.

For the women who had taken up jobs during the war and experienced the independence of working outside the home, it was a disappointing time. The majority of them had to give up their positions for the returned soldiers.

So while the end of the war was a time of loving reunions and relief from the threat of being invaded by an enemy, it was not perfect or heavenly, as many people had expected it to be.

FROM THE TIME

Historical Source

In Flanders Fields
By John McCrae, 1915

In Flanders fields the poppies blow
Between the crosses, row on row,
 That mark our place: and in the sky
 The larks, still bravely singing, fly
Scarce heard amid the guns below.

We are the Dead. Short days ago
We lived, felt dawn, saw sunset glow,
 Loved and were loved, and now we lie
 In Flanders fields.

Take up our quarrel with the foe:
To you from failing hands we throw
 The torch; be yours to hold it high.
 If ye break faith with us who die
We shall not sleep, though poppies grow
 In Flanders fields.

Many beautiful and heartbreaking poems like the one above survive
from the battlefields of World War One. They were often written by
young soldiers who didn't have much education. Yet they could write
about bravery, death, fear, friendship and sacrifice with powerful
words and haunting images that give us a picture of what war was
really like.

DID YOU KNOW HOW BALLET CAME TO AUSTRALIA?

The first proper ballet performed in Australia was called *The Fair Maid of Perth*, and it was put on at The Theatre Royal, Sydney, in January 1835.

Anna Pavlova, one of the world's most well-known ballerinas, toured Australia in 1926 and again in 1929. It was during this tour that the pavlova dessert was created in her honour.

After World War Two, many famous European ballet dancers fled their home countries and settled in Australia, starting up ballet schools and dance companies.

Some early Australian ballets created especially for our local dancers were called *Terra Australis*, *The Black Swan*, *The Outlaw*, *Corroboree* and Laurel Martyn's *Mathinna*.

The Australian Ballet was started in 1962 by a British dancer called Peggy van Praagh, and the Australian Ballet School was founded in 1964 by an English lady called Margaret Scott.

ouraustraliangirl.com.au

Want to find out more?
To play games, enter competitions and read more
about your favourite characters, visit our website.
We'd love to hear from you!

Want to find out more?

Turn the page for a
sneak peek at Book 4

Peacetime
for Alice

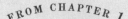

AT the greenhouse, Alice threw off Papa Sir's nightgown and shivered in her dance tunic as she wound the gramophone. It was dark and chilly, but she felt excitement tingle through her, as if she were winding herself up, too, ready for all the leaps and twirls and stretches. Though she was dying to launch straight into the longer pieces, she made herself go over and warm up on the barre, swishing her legs back and forth, rising up on her toes, sweeping her arms through the positions until her fingertips felt warm and her wrists felt soft and supple.

A sharp tap at the window made Alice

wobble in surprise. She turned to peer out into the sunrise, and against the pink sky, she saw Teddy, two steaming mugs in his hands. She ran to let him in.

'Cocoa,' he said in the flat, lifeless voice that he'd had since he came back from fighting in the Great War. 'For when you're finished. May I watch?'

'Yes,' said Alice in surprise, running to get his old painting chair from where it was folded in the corner. Teddy hadn't shown any interest in her dancing since he'd come home. If he was anywhere near when Miss Lillibet arrived, he usually lowered his head and slunk off. He hadn't shown any interest in anything, really, except sitting on the verandah and glaring at James. He didn't paint anymore, and he didn't smile. That cocoa's the nicest thing he's done since he's been back, Alice thought as she changed the gramophone record, feeling a little puzzled. I wonder why he's come?

Alice Alexander . 1919

Nellie's Quest
1850

It's 1850 and Nellie's best friend, Mary, is gravely ill. To give Mary the support she needs, Nellie must break a promise and go on a quest to find the Thompson family. But will they be able to help? And who will Nellie turn to when her own life is in danger?

Meet Nellie and join her adventures in the third of four stories about an Irish girl with a big heart, in search of the freedom to be herself.

Penny Matthews, critically acclaimed author of the Nellie books, has written junior novels, chapter books and picture books. Her novel *A Girl Like Me* was a CBCA Notable Book in 2010 and won the Sisters in Crime 2011 Davitt Award for Young Adult Fiction.

GRACE
1808

It's 1808 and Grace is living with her uncle in London. They have no money, and Grace is always lonely and often hungry. One afternoon she can't resist taking a shiny red apple from a grocer's cart – and in a split second, her life changes forever...

You can read all the books in the Grace series...

**MEET GRACE
A FRIEND FOR GRACE
GRACE AND GLORY
A HOME FOR GRACE**

LETTY
1841

It's 1841 and Letty is on the docks in England, farewelling her bossy older sister who is about to take a long sea voyage to Australia. But then there's a mix-up and Letty finds herself on the ship, too. How will she manage on the other side of the world, and what will life be like there?

You can read all the books in the Letty series...

**MEET LETTY
LETTY AND THE STRANGER'S LACE
LETTY ON THE LAND
LETTY'S CHRISTMAS**

Poppy
1864

It's 1864 and Poppy lives at Bird Creek Mission near Echuca. When her brother, Gus, runs away to pan for gold, Poppy plans her own escape ... Will she ever find Gus, whom she loves more than anything in the world?

You can read all the books in the Poppy series ...

Meet Poppy
Poppy at Summerhill
Poppy and the Thief
Poppy Comes Home

Rose
1900

It's 1900 and Rose lives with her family in a big house in Melbourne. She wants to play cricket, climb trees and be an adventurer. But Rose's mother has other ideas. Will Rose ever really get to do the things she loves?

You can read all the books in the Rose series ...

Meet Rose
Rose on Wheels
Rose's Challenge
Rose in Bloom

Follow the story of your favourite
Australian girls and you will see that there
is a special charm on the cover of each book
that tells you something about the story.

Here they all are. You can tick them
off as you read each one.

 ♥ **Meet Grace**

 ♥ **A Friend for Grace**

 ♥ **Grace and Glory**

 ♥ **A Home for Grace**

 ♥ **MEET LETTY**

 ♥ **LETTY AND THE STRANGER'S LACE**

 ♥ **LETTY ON THE LAND**

 ♥ **LETTY'S CHRISTMAS**

 ♥ *Meet Poppy*

 ♥ *Poppy at Summerhill*

 ♥ *Poppy and the Thief*

 ♥ *Poppy Comes Home*

 ♥ *Meet Rose*

 ♥ *Rose on Wheels*

 ♥ *Rose's Challenge*

 ♥ *Rose in Bloom*

 ♥ **Meet Nellie**

 ♥ **Nellie and the Secret Letter**

 ♥ **Nellie's Quest**

 ♥ **Nellie's Greatest Wish**

 ♥✓ **Meet Alice**

♥✓ **Alice and the Apple Blossom Fair**

♥✓ **Alice of Peppermint Grove**

♥ **Peacetime for Alice**